The Water-Babies
Tom in The Undersea World

Illustrations by **Virginia Smith**
based on the Animation+Live Action film
The Water-Babies.
A Peter Shaw Production.

COLLINS COLOUR CUBS

When Tom, the little chimney-sweep-turned-water-baby, took the otter's advice and headed downstream in search of the water-babies' playground it was the start of a tremendous adventure.

As Tom and Toby made their way downriver, a storm raged overhead. Thunder rolled and lightning flashed. When Tom looked up he could see the raindrops plopping on the surface of the water.

"Hey! The river's leaking!" he exclaimed.

The river tossed and tumbled them. They tried to clutch at the reeds but they were swept helplessly on.

But the storm was over at last and they found themselves in the estuary. The water was sea-coloured, clear and bright, and the sandy bottom glittered with pretty seashells.

"Och!" said a voice. "What a daft idiot!"

"Who? Me?" asked Tom, startled.

"*Me*!" said the voice. "It's me I'm talkin' aboot! A right dafty! That's what I am! Swum these waters these last umpteen years, and look at me noo! Trapped!"

The voice belonged to a lobster. A big Scots lobster wearing a tam-o'-shanter. The lobster caught sight of Tom. "And whit are *you* starin' at?" he asked.

"Er, I was wondering," said Tom, "what that is you're holding on to?"

"Holdin' on to!" screamed the lobster. "You daft thing! Do you no' see it's holdin' on to me?"

"Maybe I could free you," suggested Tom.

"*You* free me!" exclaimed the lobster. "That's downright offensive, that is! A wee shuggie like you!"

The lobster paused and looked at Tom, then waggled his tam-o'-shanter in a more friendly way.

"Ah, well, maybe you could at that. Come on then, give us a hand!"

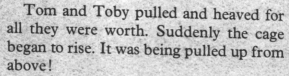

Tom and Toby pulled and heaved for all they were worth. Suddenly the cage began to rise. It was being pulled up from above!

"All's lost!" wailed Jock, the lobster. "I'm theirs! They'll boil me and garnish me!"

"Oh, one last try!" said Tom.

"A' right, laddie," said Jock. "*Heave*! PIPECLAY UP THE LUM!"

Just as the lobster-pot broke surface the bar cracked and Jock fell out.

"Aw! You saved my life, laddie!" said Jock. "What's your name, laddie?"

"Tom," said Tom.

"Give us your hand, Tom!" said Jock. "We'll away doon deep and you can tell me your story." And the three of them swam down to the sandy bottom.

"Water-babies?" said Jock when he'd listened to Tom. "Aye, I've heard tell o' them. In the Middle Ocean, that's where they are. Man, I've heard it's a great place to be!"

"But where is it?" asked Tom.

"Well, it's ower far for a wee soul like you to be goin' by yoursel'. There's the dangers o' the deep—and the worst o' them is that terrible Killer Shark! Roams the seas, he does, lookin' for water-babies. Enslaves them! Takes them to Shark Castle. Oh, I hear it's terrible!"

"I've just got to find them," said Tom, "if I'm ever to get back Up There to Ellie."

"You'll no' do it by your wee silly self," said Jock. "You'll need a strong, intelligent sort o' chap to go along wi' ye."

"You mean *you'll* come?" shouted Tom. "*High cockolorum!*"

"What's yon?" asked Jock.

"Well, for me it's plenty to eat and a warm place to sleep and, oh, lots of things. . . ."

"I ken fine what you mean," said Jock,
bursting into song.

> High cockolorum
> Means lots o' things to me.
> A Saturday night in Glasgow
> Wi' a lassie on my knee.

The swirl o' the kilt
And the magic lilt
O' a Highland pipe and drum.

It's really grand
Och! ye understand
It's pipeclay up the lum!

It's Scots Wha Hae
It's Hogmanay
It's high cockolorum!

And they both sang as off they swaggered.

> Friends for ever
> Sticking together
> High cockolorum!
> Hey, hey, hey, we're on our way!
> HIGH COCK-O-LORUM!

They swam a long way, through dark, weedy depths, past rainbow-coloured fish, amongst the rotting timbers of sunken ships, but never a sign of a water-baby.

"What's that?" said Tom in a fright. Screeches of eerie laughter echoed through the sunken galleon.

"Losh!" said Jock. "It must be The Haunter!"

"Hello!" said a musical voice. "Bet you were frightened just then!"

"Some was, some wasn't!" said Jock
huffily.

"Blimey! It's a seahorse!" exclaimed
Tom.

"Pleased to see you anyway!" said
Terence, the seahorse. "What brings you
to these parts?"

"I'm looking for the water-babies,"
said Tom.

"Oh, I know about *them*," said Terence. "I hear them singing sometimes."

"Really! Could you show us the way?" asked Tom eagerly.

"Love to," said Terence. "Tired of being here on my own."

"High cockolorum!" sang Tom.

"Oh . . . high cockolorum!" sang Terence.

"High cockolorum!" sang Jock, and they set off arm in arm.

They walked for a bit, and they swam for a bit, and they walked again on the sea bottom.

They had come a long way, and now
they were in amongst some dark, creepy
trees with waving branches that seemed
to reach out towards them.

"Take them," commanded a rasping voice and slimy tentacles wrapped themselves around the three friends.

"It's the Killer Shark!" yelled Jock.

"Keep away from me!" shouted Tom. "Help! Somebody!"

"Do I 'ear *a* cry for 'elp?" answered a voice with a French accent. "Never fear! Claude is 'ere!" And a swordfish swam into view.

The evil trees retreated in terror as Claude dived into the attack.

"Ah, what an *aventure*!" he exclaimed,
slashing to left and right.

"He's done it!" exclaimed Tom. "We're
free! High cockolorum!"

"'igh cockolorum!" said Claude.

"Best be gettin' on our way," warned
Jock, "or yon shark'll get to the water-
babies before us."

"My sword ees at your command!"
said Claude with a flourish.

"We *must* find them because they're the only ones who can tell me how to get back Up There where Ellie is," said Tom.

The water darkened except for a bright glow which gradually changed into the beautiful face of Mrs Doasyouwouldbedoneby, the good fairy who looked after Tom.

They looked again into the dazzling light and now they saw the water-babies. Shark guards were driving them into the dungeons of Shark Castle.

The picture faded but the light led them on until they found themselves in the water-babies' playground.

It was true, what they had seen in the bright sphere. All the water-babies, except one, had been captured.

"You must help me!" sobbed Ariadne.

"But *I* came here to *get* help," said Tom. ". . . help to get back Up There where I belong."

"Then you must go to The Kraken," said Ariadne. "He can help you *and* the water-babies."

"The who . . .?" asked Tom.

"The Kraken. He is Lord of the Ocean and he lives at the Other End of Nowhere," said Ariadne.

"Crikey! How do I get there?" exclaimed Tom.

"Through the cave," said Ariadne. "It's the only way."

The cave led into a tunnel and the tunnel led out into icy wastes and frozen seas. As they looked, a crystal ladder came down from nowhere and stopped at Tom's feet.

"Ladders are for climbing," said Tom. "Let's go!" Then, "Hey," he said, "there's air at the top! Only Toby and I can breathe air. It'll 'ave to be us on our tod!"

Tom and Toby clung to the ladder and it whizzed up the ice chimney.

They stepped off into a vast ice hall.

"Woof!" barked Toby as icy blasts hit him.

Suddenly Tom was dangling from a great furry paw.

"Trespassers will be petrified," said a deep, polar bear voice.

"I demand to see The Kraken!" said Tom.

"Ho! ho! ho!" laughed the polar bear. "A young tearaway!

"Demand—is it?" he said. "Well, if you aren't afraid of me perhaps you won't be afraid of his lordship, either. Come along!"

The polar bear took Tom's hand in a friendly grasp and led him through corridors with walls of ice and high, arched roofs.

Guarding a door at the end of one of those passages was a walrus.

"'lo, Cyril," said the polar bear.

"'lo, Archie," said the walrus. "What's this, then?"

"Young feller wants to see The Kraken."

"He'll have to wait," said Cyril.

"But how long?" asked Tom.

"Till I say so," grumbled the walrus.

But Tom didn't wait. He and Toby
were through the ice door and into the
ice lift quicker than Cyril could call
Stop!

The ice lift dazzled with crystals.

"It's like the 'all of mirrors!" said Tom.
"It must be *some* place this old Kraken's
got!"

They stepped out into the coldest, iciest landscape you could ever imagine: mountains of ice and frozen seas for as far as Tom could see.

"Look, Toby!" said Tom. "This must be the Other End of Nowhere!"

As they looked, a great shining globe came out of the grey sky. It was coming straight towards them, growing bigger all the time.

It came to rest in a flurry of white mist. From the centre of the sphere a loud, harsh voice boomed and echoed.

"Some call me Neptune, Father of the Seas, but most know me as THE KRAKEN—THE EARTH SHAKER."

"Not many know me at all," said Tom in a small voice. "I'm just Tom."

"Unknown, uninvited!" said The Kraken. "Explain!"

"Well, it's the water-babies, see, they've been captured and I've just got to rescue them . . . and I want to know how to get back to Ellie, Up There, where I come from, and . . ."

"So!" boomed the voice of The Kraken. "Two requests! One only, land-child. Choose!" And The Kraken threw down a crystal sphere.

When Tom looked into it he saw Shark Castle, the imprisoned, unhappy water-babies and their cruel shark guards. Tom could not bear the sight.

"Please, set the water-babies free!" he pleaded.

"So be it!" said The Kraken. "Now go! I put you to the test. You must defeat the Killer Shark."

"What, by meself?" gasped Tom.

Lightning flashed from The Kraken's sword as the sphere went back into the icy mists. The Kraken's voice was faint but clear: "I shall be watching. I shall be helping."

Cyril and Archie were waiting at the bottom of the ice lift when Tom and Toby got out.

"You've got to help me to beat the Killer Shark," said Tom.

"It can't be done . . ." said Archie.

"The Kraken says I *must*," said Tom.

". . . without a bit of planning," said Cyril, starting to feel quite friendly towards Tom.

So they put their heads together and came up with a plan.

"Do you think we can do it?" asked Tom.

"'course we can," said Archie.

Shark Castle looked dark and gloomy as they approached.

But the bombardment seemed to have begun! They could hear thunderous crashing noises as large icicles smashed into the towers.

Tom's underwater friends were wasting no time. Claude was zipping off the icicles from the underside of the iceberg and sending them crashing down on the castle. Tom could see them from the top of the iceberg.

"Our turn, now!" he called.

Archie's relatives had come to help and they were rolling huge ice snowballs towards the edge. Down they went, one after another, smashing through the walls of Shark Castle.

The sharks were in a frenzy as the ice snowballs crashed down upon them.

They had left the water-babies unguarded.

"Never fear. Claude is 'ere," said a voice, and the swordfish slashed through the bars of the dungeon.

The water-babies were free!

"Hurry!" called Tom. "This way, all of you!"

"Aye, get a move on there!" commanded Jock. "Look slippy, the lot of ye. The sharks are at your backs."

And so they were. But so was Claude.

"Sharks to the rear!" yelled Tom.

"Arrr! Fighting-time!" sang Claude with glee. "Back, you cowards, or the Chevalier Claude will slice you into little pieces!"

When all the sharks had retreated inside the castle, Tom and Jock had their cleverest idea of the whole battle. They dropped the portcullis gate and trapped the sharks inside. They were prisoners in their own castle!

The land friends and the undersea
friends met by the pool at the top of the
iceberg. "We did it!" they cried.

The water-babies cheered. "Thanks,
everybody! Thank you, Tom!"

"PIPECLAY UP THE LUM!" yelled
Jock.

ISBN 0 00 123503 6
Copyright © 1978 Ariadne Films Ltd.
A Peter Shaw Production
Based on Charles Kingsley's classic story
Illustrations and text Copyright © 1978 William Collins Sons & Co. Ltd.
Lyrics from the song "High Cockolorum"
Copyright © 1978 Babies Music Publishing Ltd.
Printed and made in Great Britain